THE INVINCIBLE TONY SPEARS

and the BRILLIANT BLOB

Neal Layton

TONY SPEARS
THE BUTTON
THE SIGN
PRESS THIS BUTTON
TO INITIATE
PROCEDURES OF
COFF
TEA

1. ALL CHANGE

Things had been going really well for Tony
Spears.

OK, so the year hadn't started too well
when he had moved house, and started a new
school mid-term – that had made him a bit
miserable, but when he found 'the button' in
his kitchen cupboard, things began to look up.
Pretty high up, actually.

The button could transport him from

VIA HYPER-LIFT

the kitchen of his new flat to the flight deck of the *Invincible*, a type 1AA spaceship capable of planetary, galactic and other forms of dimensional travel.

After that, he befriended an alien race of telepathic rabbits, saved the people of Earth from being eaten by a Gatorilla*, and restored peace to the planet Xo49p using huge amounts of bubblegum. To top it all off, he even won an award at his new school.

* Footnote - Gatorilla. Planet of origin - Xo49p. Danger level - High

Tony had got used to Mum's new friend, Chris, coming round for dinner, or helping paint their hall. I mean, he had made new friends at school, so it was only fair that his mum should have new friends too. But one day when they were having tea together, Tony realised something big was about to happen.

Chris had taken them to Tony's favourite cafe.

'Tony,' began Chris. 'Your mum and I
have known each other for quite a while now,
haven't we … and you know we like each other
very much, don't you …'

'Mmm,' mumbled Tony as he picked out
gherkins from his bun and munched them into
star and moon shapes.

'Well, er …'

'Tony, what Chris is trying to say, is that I'm going to have a baby … we're going to have a baby. A little brother or sister … for you.'

At this point Tony nearly choked on a chip.

A baby…?!

Tony chewed and chewed on that chip. Whilst he chewed, Chris and Tony's mum sat there beaming at him, waiting for a reaction, until Tony said, 'Umm, wow, that's great, Mum … and Chris.'

After Chris paid the bill, it was time to leave and Tony's mum said, 'I've got a few things to do in town now, Tony, but Chris has to go home to work on his van. Would you like to come along with me, or do you want go back with him to play before bath time?'

'Thanks, Mum, perhaps I'll leave you to it and see you later ...'

As soon as he got though the front door of their flat Tony knew what he had to do ... he went straight to the kitchen, opened the cupboard, moved a few plates so he could see the button and pressed it, CLICK.

In seconds, his kitchen had transformed into a hyper-lift and transported him to the bunker where his spaceship, the *Invincible,* was kept.

CLICK!

The Computer whirred into life.

'Launch procedures initiated. Lift-off in T minus 20 seconds. Please take your seat, Master Spears.'

10

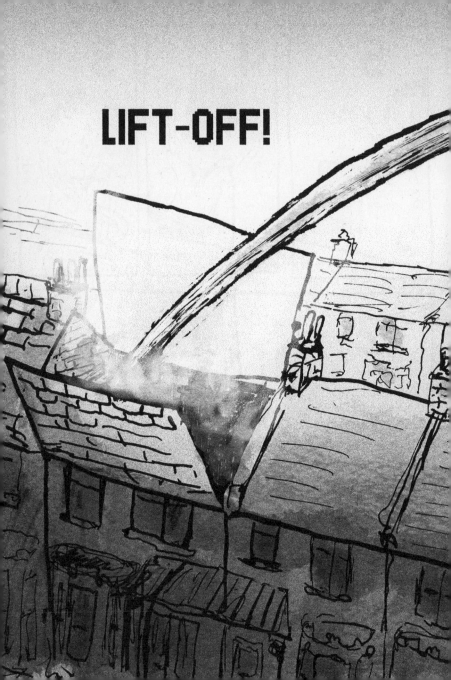

2. DOT

After flicking more switches and buttons, he
was soon soaring high above the rooftops.
Quite quickly the town dropped away,
disappearing into the curve of the Earth,

until the Earth, too, shrank from a big blue orb
to nothing, disappearing completely as Tony's
journey took him further and further into
outer space.

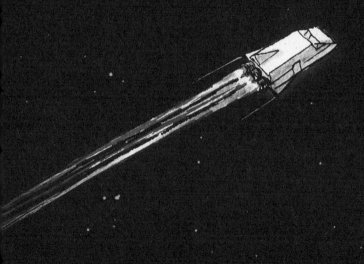

Tony didn't know where he was going. He just wanted to go somewhere, anywhere that was far away. He found the feeling of moving soothing as planets and stars zipped past the viewing

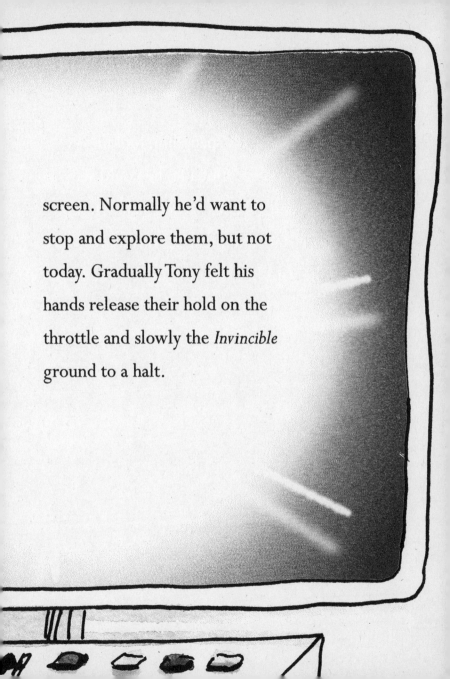

screen. Normally he'd want to stop and explore them, but not today. Gradually Tony felt his hands release their hold on the throttle and slowly the *Invincible* ground to a halt.

Tony sat inside his spaceship, looking at the viewing screen. Outside, he could see stars, planets and galaxies – each galaxy full of billions more stars and planets. Tony's eyes were drawn to the gaps between the light – the huge emptiness.

'Are you all right, Master Spears? You seem to be headed somewhere with great purpose. If you tell me your destination, I can set a course and give you an estimated time of arrival, though I have to say we are now in a distant nebula. There isn't anything of interest to be found in this corner of the multiverse.'

'What's a nebula?'

'It's where stars are born, a star nursery if you like.'

'Oh. Computer, I just want to be alone. I

don't know why, I just want to.'

'Affirmative, Master Spears. If that is your intention then you have found a perfect spot — the nearest planetary systems are squillions of space miles from here.'

Whilst he sat there, staring at the
squillions of space miles, something strange
shimmered past the screen, close up.

'What was that? There it is again!
Computer, did you see it too?

'Yes, Tony, my sensors are registering a
lifeform outside the ship. It is small and
fast-moving and does not correspond to
anything stored in my information bank. This
is most unexpected.'

As Tony spoke, the little flitting object
came close to the viewing port, hovering
outside for a while, before whizzing away into
the darkness of space.

It was about the size of an orange, but sort of see-through, very much like some of the sea creatures Tony had seen on TV. Although it was round, its shape wobbled like a bubble, glowing bright blue and green against the inky blackness of space. But the thing that amazed Tony most about it was its eyes. As it hovered at the window, all three of them stared deep into Tony's own eyes. Tony could not forget that look. He felt like it went deep inside him, as if the blob was desperately trying to tell him something, before it turned and whizzed off again.

'Computer, that thing, whatever it is, I think it's very frightened.'

The big problem was what to do next. Looking at the display above the viewing screen, Tony could see that it was nearly 6.45 p.m. Earth time and, being at the outer reaches of the multiverse, he would have to start flying home soon to get back in time for his bath. Even at super-duper speed that would take at least twenty minutes. He didn't want to arrive home late, but somehow it felt wrong to leave the 'blob', whatever it was, out here all alone in the dark.

'Computer, are you *sure* you don't know what it is?'

'I am positive, Tony. I have cross-referenced it with all known lifeforms on record. Whatever that thing is, it has never been seen before.'

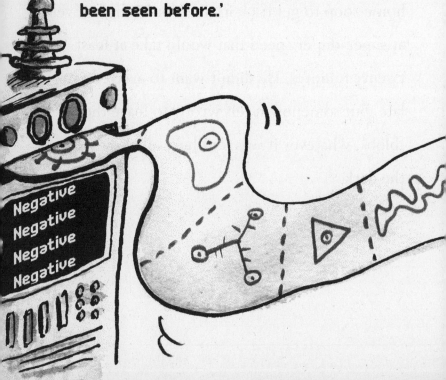

As Tony stared out, the blob began flitting around and around the outside of his spaceship.

'I don't think we should leave it out here. I can't explain it but … I think it needs help.'

'Tony, I do not understand why you think it needs help. It has not communicated with you.'

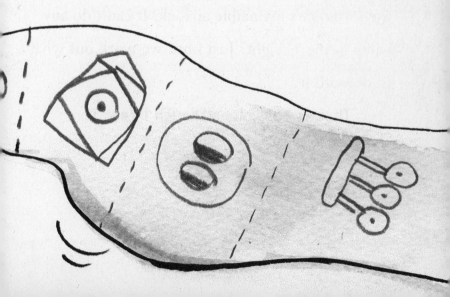

'Well, not exactly, but it looked at me …
with a certain kind of look.'

'Tony, I would advise against capturing
the blob. Although it would be an impressive
scientific discovery, we have no idea what
it is, or what its intentions are. It could be
dangerous.'

'OK, Computer, well how about we put it in
the *Invincible*'s invincible airlock? It can't do any
harm in there, right? Just until we work out what
to do with it.'

'That is possible, although I fear it

won't want to enter the airlock of its own accord.'

'Well, I'll usher it in and show it I mean no harm. I think it likes me.'

'How can you tell that, Tony?'

'It's just a feeling, the way it looked at me with those eyes.'

32

'This is not logical.'

Tony pressed his face to the viewing
screen. Outside, the glowing blob hovered.

'Computer, I have to do something!'

'But Master Spears—'

'Computer, please open the outer airlock.'

'Tony, I do not agree with this course
of action.'

'Computer, please open the airlock. I don't
want to let it into the cabin, but we can keep it
in the airlock corridor until we work out what
to do with it. Whatever it is, it needs help.

I know it does. Open the airlock – that is an order.'

'Affirmative, Master Spears. Opening outer airlock now.'

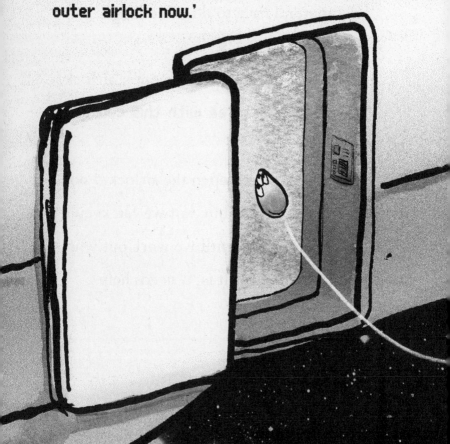

With a hiss of compressed gas, the hull door slid out and to one side. The blob whizzed round and round in circles three times before shooting inside.

'Right, Computer, please close the outside airlock door but keep the inner one closed. We can hold the 'blob' there until we get back to Earth.'

'Affirmative, Master Spears.'

Tony walked across the bridge and down the stairs to the lower airlock door.

It was it this point that Tony was glad he was aboard the *Invincible*. The ship had been given that name for a reason it was as — its name implied, totally invincible. Once Tony was inside, as long as all windows and doors were shut, he was completely safe from anything, even unknown alien lifeforms.

Peering through the safety glass of the interior door, he could see the blob flitting about. Suddenly the door lights began to flash green.

'Computer, what's happening, I told you the inside door must remain SHUT.'

38

'Tony, the door seems to have been activated by some unknown source. The blob will gain access to the inside of the space ship in 10, 9, 8, 7 seconds. Tony, please remove yourself immediately.'

But it was too late. The door to the cabin hiss-clunked open and in a flash the blob shot inside, bouncing round the bridge like a ball in a game of ping-pong.

'Aghhh!'

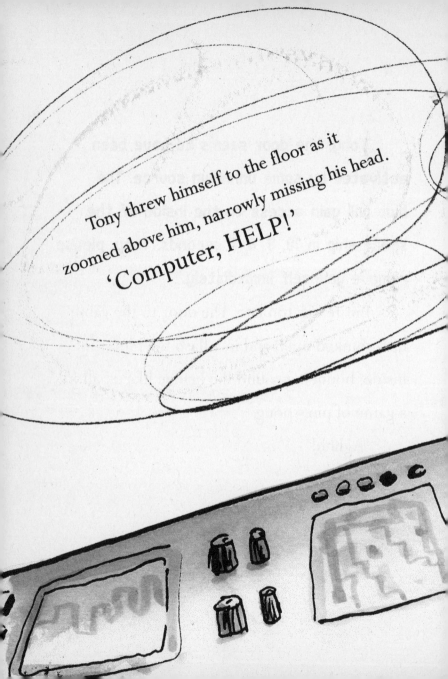

Tony threw himself to the floor as it zoomed above him, narrowly missing his head.

'Computer, HELP!'

3. IN A JAR

It only took nineteen minutes to return home, but to Tony it felt a lot longer. He spent nearly the whole journey ducking for cover, or turning off the many alarms which the blob had set off. It wasn't until they neared the glow of Earth's solar system that it began to calm down.

'There, there. That's it. I'm not going to hurt you. You're safe now. There's no need to dot about. You're safe now, my little friend. Yes, that seems to fit you, doesn't it? Dot … that's what I'll call you.'

After a quick journey by hyper-lift, Tony
was back in his kitchen, gingerly cradling the
blob now called 'Dot' in his hands. He
had kept all sorts of pets before —
caterpillars, ants, worms —
but never an alien life
form.

As he entered the kitchen, Dot kept
rolling from one hand to another, a bit like the
furry caterpillar toys he'd seen at the fair. In
the bright lights of his kitchen it had gone
very see through, with just a warm
pin-pricking feeling across his
hands to remind him it was
still there.

Tony could hear Chris, still working on his van outside. His mum would be back any minute, and then it would be bath time. *Still time for a quick snack,* thought Tony. After all that space travel, he was hungry!

But what should he do with Dot? He would need somewhere to keep it.

In one of the cupboards he found a plastic jar with a lid. He slid Dot into it, popped the lid on top and punched holes in the lid with a fork to let air inside.

Then Tony set the jar on the sideboard

whilst he investigated the kitchen cupboards.

Peanut butter, bread — right, where's the honey?

Looking over his shoulder, he noticed Dot flitting round the plastic jar. Dot's whizzing about was getting so wild the jar began to bounce about.

'Woah! You want my attention, don't you? Well, OK, you've got it ... What do you want?'

Tony held his half-munched sandwich in one hand while he lifted the lid with the other to peep in. Immediately Dot zipped out through the tiny gap and started circling Tony.

49

'What? You want a sandwich too? Don't be daft. Aliens don't eat peanut butter sandwiches, do they? C'mon, if you're hungry, lets go to the fridge and see what you might like ...'

Cheese, milk, cabbage ...

As Tony opened the fridge, the door light came on and Dot suddenly ZOOOOOMED in.

'Crumbs, you were hungry, but I don't know what you're —'

52

Tony stopped. Dot hadn't made for any of the food in there. Instead it had flattened itself into a lozenge shape covering the door light, and as it did so its skin started to flow with rainbow colours like a drop of oil on water. The door light dimmed and went out. And the strip lights on the ceiling flickered.

Dot started pulsing.

'So that's what you eat — you eat light! Well, I guess you are an alien of unknown origin ...' laughed Tony.

He pulled up a stool and finished his sandwich as Dot pulsed and flowed in the fridge. The lights flickered again.

Just then Tony heard his mum's footsteps coming up the hall and the familiar sound of 'Tony... time for your bath.'

Bath time was not one of Tony's favourite parts of the day, but surely sharing it with an alien would make it more fun. He wondered if Dot needed a bath too. Dot seemed to have calmed down after its snack and Tony was glad. He wasn't sure how he'd explain a glowing blob bouncing about the bathroom if his mum came in, so he gently set the plastic jar on the floor whilst he got washed, and hoped it wouldn't get lively again.

Later, in bed with the lights out, he noticed Dot had returned to the brilliant colours he'd seen in space. But just as he was about to fall asleep, the jar started bouncing around again.

Tony drearily leaned out of bed and creaked the
lid open, only to have Dot whizz out and start
ZOOOOOOMING around his room.

'Dot! Shh! Calm down, will you … Look, it's bedtime, the time when we go to bed … and sleep. It's been a tiring day.'

Even aliens must need to sleep, thought Tony.

But Dot started to pulsate even faster. Its colours were changing, too, from yellows and oranges to blues and purples, and the surface of its skin was rippling.

Tony grabbed his communicator, and pressed the transmit button.

'Computer, are you there? I have a problem, I need help!'

'Affirmative, Master Spears. I have been monitoring the alien lifeform you call Dot closely since its arrival on Earth — its energy levels are rising ...'

'It's in trouble. What should I do? Computer, please HELP ME!'

Tony reached out his hands towards Dot. The surface of its skin had changed from ripples to spikes like a sea urchin, its colours flashing between purple and crimson, getting brighter and brighter.

'Master Spears, please move away — the levels are spiking dramatically. Danger, Master Spears,

DANGER!'

Tony threw his hands over his face. Dot's colours were now too bright to look at.

Until . . .

SPPLLLLLLLLEEEEEEEEECCCCCHHHH!
Large blobs of goop sprayed out of its spikes all over Tony.

When he removed his hands they were covered in glittery - sticky - stuff that smelt of wet socks and burnt cooking. Tony noticed that Dot's skin had returned to smooth yellows and oranges. It slid across the floor and bounced up and into the plastic jar.

'Well what was THAT all about?' stammered Tony. 'And what *is* this stuff?!'

His communicator crackled into life again.

'Master Spears, I suspect Dot has just emitted some waste.'

'What do you mean?'

'Much the same as all humans do, I suspect that Dot has just been to the toilet.'

'A POO?!' exclaimed Tony.

'Exactly, Master Spears. And judging by its current spectral vibrations, it feels a lot better now.'

'I think I need another bath …' mumbled Tony.

4. THE SCHOOL PROJECT

Thankfully the rest of the night was uneventful. Dot spent it sleeping in the jar. And Tony slept soundly too.

But the next morning at breakfast, as Tony made his way to the fridge to grab some milk for his astro cereal, something made him stop in his tracks. Pinned to the fridge door was a weird black and white image of a frightening-looking alien creature, a different one to Dot.

'Mum! What's THIS?!'

Tony's mum looked up from making the sandwiches for Tony's packed lunch.

'Oh, yes, Tony, this is the first photo of your new brother or sister! I went for a scan yesterday and they gave me this print-out.'

Tony looked at the fuzzy dots printed on the scrap of paper attached to the door. It didn't look like anything Tony had ever seen before.

'Are you sure that's a baby?'

'Yes, of course, Tony. It's a very healthy-looking baby. Anyway,' said his mum, pointing at Tony's jar. 'What's that for? It looks interesting. Is it for a school project?'

'Oh, um. Yeah, sort of …'

And he popped the jar under the table while he ate his breakfast. This was a lot to take in.

Tony didn't know what to do with Dot, so he left it in the jar and put it in his school bag, packing a few pairs of sport socks around it so the jar didn't break. Tony hoped Dot wouldn't mind the noise of a busy classroom.

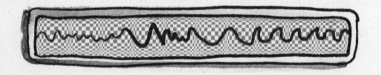

Special
Research
Project

'Right, children,' said Mr Simpson. 'Quiet please. Now, for the remainder of this term you will all be working on a special research project of *your* choice. Choose something you're interested in learning about, or perhaps something that's going on in your family at the moment. And make sure it's something you are *really* interested in because this project will run right through the whole term. We can spend the rest of the lesson on the computers deciding on your individual topics. There's one work station each. And at the end of the lesson

I'll collect up your project titles.'

As the rest of the class chattered their way to the ICT section, Tony found a free computer and sat down.

He couldn't get the image of the baby scan out of his head. Was that really his brother or sister? It didn't look like anything human at all, more like some kind of weird alien creature. With a quick glance over his shoulder, Tony typed in: BABY SCAN LOOKS LIKE AN ALIEN.

Almost instantly, streams of pictures like the one on his fridge filled the screen. Tony picked an interesting-looking one that had arrows on it and clicked … And then clicked again, enlarging the image showing the arrows pointing to different things in the fuzzy dots — head, eyes, hands, feet, spine.

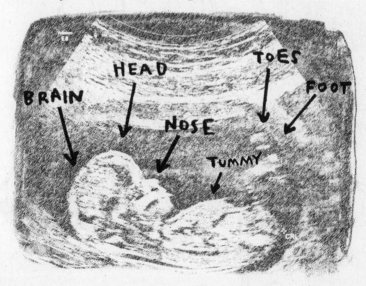

It looked more like something he'd find on one of his intergalactic adventures in the *Invincible*. Surely that couldn't be a baby?!

74

Tony was so engrossed in what he was doing, he didn't hear Mr Simpson say, 'Last five minutes now, everyone.' And later, when he suddenly realised Mr Simpson was standing behind him looking over his shoulder, he nearly jumped out of his skin.

'Right, Tony. What's this you're looking at? Babies, yes, that's a great idea. And a little birdie tells me that you're about to have a new addition to your family soon.'

'B-but—' stuttered Tony.

'Excellent,' carried on Mr Simpson. 'We

nearly have all your topics now and there are some great ones already. Brian has chosen tanks, Bertrand has chosen super-fast-space-rockets, and Tony here has chosen babies.

'N—' Tony said, but before he could stammer out a proper reply another hand in the classroom shot up.

'But SIR!'

'Yes, Chandra. Do you have a question?'

'I wanted to do babies for my project, sir.'

'Oh, I see. Hmm … Well, yes, I suppose you could both choose the same topic. Or better still, why don't you collaborate and do a joint presentation? Yes, that's a much better idea. That way you can share the researching. Great, that's settled, then. Tony and Chandra will have babies as their joint project! Yes, I think we'll have a lot of fun this term. And in case you've forgotten, as if these projects aren't exciting enough, on the last day of school, after your presentations, we have our annual fancy dress school disco!'

The class cheered.

Chandra looked over to Tony and smiled.

Tony looked back at Chandra and scowled.

This was not going well. Not only had he ended up doing a project about babies but, even worse, he'd ended up doing it with a girl partner.

5. ASTROSNAX

After that, Tony couldn't seem to get away from babies. They seemed to be EVERYWHERE! Babies, babies, BABIES! Why was everyone going so goofy over BABIES?

Tony would get to school and Chandra would be sitting at his desk, waiting.

'Tony, look what I've got! Mrs Whiting has lent me some baby magazines. I thought we could cut some of the pictures out for our school project. And perhaps if we have any left over you could take them home to your mum.'

Tony looked at the magazines spread across the desk — a sea of pink and blue with big beaming eyes and toothless grins. And when he got home it would be more of the same.

'Look, Tony, see what I've bought today,
it's a baby suit for your new brother or sister,
it's covered in pink and blue rabbits so it will
suit a boy or girl. Isn't it lovely, it even has ears
and a little tail at the back.'

Even the walk to and from school seemed
to be full of babies. In prams, slings, adverts
in the shop windows. Occasionally, mums
and dads that knew him would look up from
pushing buggies and say things like, 'Hi, Tony,
not long now, eh, and you'll have one of these
in your house too!'

And ICT, which used to be one of Tony's favourite subjects, was full of babies whilst he did research for his project with Chandra.

83

All of this baby talk meant Tony enjoyed his special time with Dot even more.

Galaxy tag was their favourite game to play together.

Tony would launch the *Invincible* blasting away from planet Earth into space while Dot danced in and out of the jet stream, chasing

him all the way. And then the game would swap, and Tony would chase Dot about in space. It was great fun but the whole thing mystified the Computer.

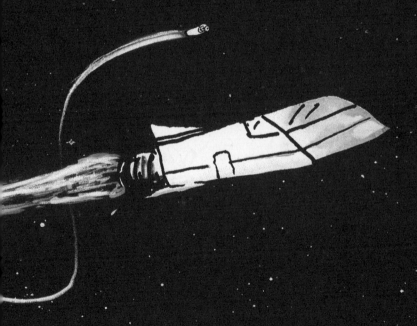

'Master Spears, may I ask you a question? I sense these interactions with Dot make you happy — you seem to enjoy the time spent with it engaging in these pointless excursions, but I do not understand why.'

'It's called playing, Computer. Dot and I are playing. Y'know … games.'

'I do not understand. What games? You have not communicated what game you are playing with Dot. How does it know the rules of the game?'

'We're just having fun, Computer. Chasing each other about, y'know, playing tag. Everybody knows how to play tag.'

'But Dot is an alien. How has it learnt how to play your game tag?'

'It's hard to explain. We're communicating,

but not with words or anything, just with feelings. Look, see here … I can tell Dot wants to play again …' And Tony grabbed the joystick. 'Computer, manual control please.'

As they zoomed off, Dot immediately followed, weaving around and around Tony's ship …

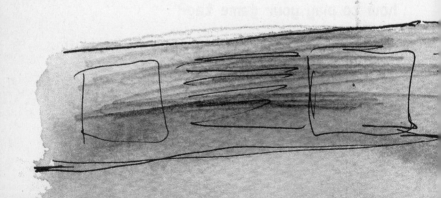

'Are you enjoying this, Dot? I certainly am!' said Tony with a big grin on his face.

But Tony was having so much fun he hadn't been paying attention to where he was flying, and passed very close to a large star …

Had Tony been in a normal spaceship, he would have been fried to a crisp, but because Tony was flying the *Invincible*, he passed almost through the centre of the star with not a scorch mark on him.

He span the controls round to face Dot, who was following close behind, dotting and weaving.

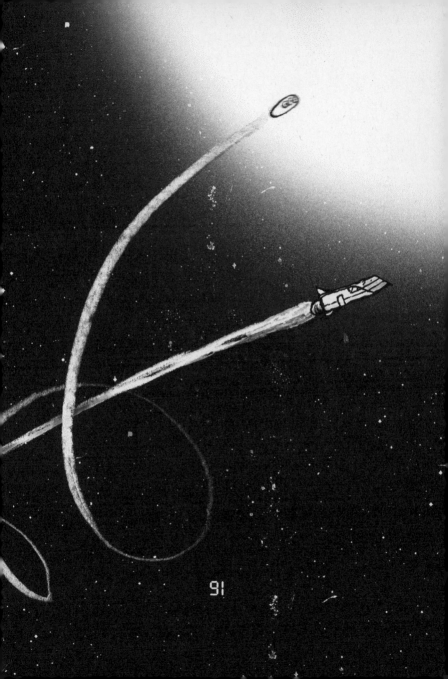

91

'Don't go too near the star, Dot. Stars are dangerous, don't you know that, Dot? They are hot, very HOT!'

But Dot carried on following the course Tony took – if anything, heading even more directly into the centre of the star, until it had completely disappeared …

'Dot, DOT! NO!' Tony was beside himself.

'He's gone, Computer. Gone forever. We were having such fun. How could this happen? It's my fault, I should have taught it …'

'Tony, wait ... I am still tracking dot's progress into the star. Remember, we do not know what it is, and what it is capable of. Any other lifeform in the known universe would have melted by now. But it is still present and now seems to have stopped in the centre of the star, the hottest place.'

'What? How?'

Suddenly the star started began to flicker, like a light bulb, until, – *pfffffff$t$* – its glow dulled to a dim white.

'Computer, where's Dot?'

'It has exited the star safely.'

Tony zoomed the viewer screen in. And in space, glowing bright orange, was Dot.

Tony became very thoughtful.

'Computer, did Dot do that? I mean, did he change that that star?'

'It appears so, Master Spears. The star underwent a massive loss of energy and is now near the end of its lifecycle.'

'What, you mean that star almost died?'

'That is correct, Master Spears.'

'I've been thinking, Computer. Dot won't be able to stay with me forever, will it?'

'I fear not, Tony.'

'Then what should I do?'

'I cannot advise, Tony. Since the alien lifeform you call Dot is completely unknown, I have nothing to reference in my data banks. I'm afraid you will have to form a plan by yourself.'

Tony returned to Earth with Dot chasing behind him.

A plan, mused Tony. *Yes, that's what I need, some kind of plan …*

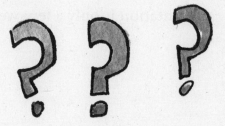

6. WE NEED A PLAN

'We need a plan!' said Chandra in school the next day. She was becoming increasingly fed up with Tony.

'I know,' mumbled Tony. 'Yes, I do need a plan.'

'Not you, we! WE need a plan. We are working on this project together, aren't we, Tony? The presentation is only a few weeks away now.'

'Yes, sorry, I was thinking about something else ... Well, we could cut out these baby pictures and stick them onto big sheets of paper,' suggested Tony.

'Hmm … well, that would be OK, but Brian has made a life-sized Sherman tank out of cardboard boxes, AND he's painted it green. Bertrand is going to bring in a rocket, a real one that will fly higher than the school. I think we need something exciting too. There's two of us working on this, we should be able to come up with something!'

'Yeah, we just need something …'

'Look, Tony, you seem very distracted. I know you've got a lot going on at the moment.'

Tony had become increasingly concerned

about Dot. He had this feeling it was getting bigger, not by much, but it didn't fit into its jar very easily any more.

As if it knew he was thinking about it, Dot suddenly started wriggling about in the school bag slung over his shoulder, and every time it wiggled, little bursts light would zap out of the flap, giving Tony the sensation of someone tickling his spine with a feather.

'Look, Tony, I've enough of this. Can you tell me exactly WHAT your problem is?' continued Chandra. 'Is it me?'

'No, I like you.'

Dot began wriggling even more.

'Is it our project, is it babies? Everybody was a baby once. Even you, Tony! Not so long ago, you couldn't talk so you cried and made cute faces and did anything you could to try and tell your mummy what you wanted…'

Tony stood there listening to Chandra. And

suddenly images of thousands of babies filled his head, all different shapes and sizes and colours. And not just children, animals too – lion cubs, chicks, calves, pups … a world FULL of tiny baby faces looking lovingly up at their mothers, cheeping, bleating, and squawking for help.

But by now Dot's wiggling, zapping, and tickling had become almost unbearable.

'I'm sorry, Chandra, I have to go quickly … um, to the toilet.' Tony giggled. And he darted up out of his seat, towards the classroom door

Mr Simspon looked up in surprise and Chandra said, 'I think Tony needed the loo, he looked desperate.'

As soon as Hubert heard this, he burst out in guffaws of laughter.

Tony pelted down the corridor, swerving

into the toilets with the door closing behind him. Thankfully, because it was lesson time, they were empty.

'Dot, please settle down whilst I talk to you. Listen … Dot, are you listening to me?'

As Tony opened his bag and found the remains of the plastic jar, Dot flew out and started bouncing about in a very agitated way.

'Firstly, about this stars thing. You just can't go round eating stars. Planets like ours need them. And secondly, if you come to school with me, you have to behave yourself, OK?

I just can't play all the time; I need to work too.'

   But as he talked Tony noticed there seemed
something different about Dot's body.

It was stretching like a water balloon until, with the squirting sound of a squeezy tomato ketchup bottle, its body squelched into four blobs.

Tony sat and stared. It was just like someone had performed a magic trick right before his eyes. One second, there was one Dot, and now there were four, spinning round and round. Faster and faster …

… until with another sound, like water going down a plughole, the spinning stopped. And floating before Tony was not four Dots but one again, a MUCH bigger one. Dangling underneath it were four long legs that looked like jelly sweets, and at the end of each leg was another eye.

Tony was speechless.

As if in answer to Tony's silence, his communicator bleeped.

'Tony, are you there? What's going on?'

Dot started pulsing different colours and then flew over to the hand dryers. Suddenly all the toilets started flushing, the taps started running into and over the sinks, and the hand dryers whirred on and off and on and off and on and off, until all the lights in the whole school went out.

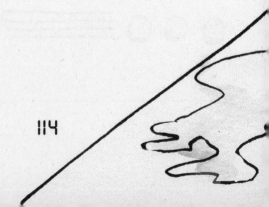

Tony ran out into the corridor. By now he could hear gasps from all over the school as doors opened and teachers poked their heads out. But before he got through the door of his classroom, he met Mr Simpson and the rest of his class coming out.

'Ahh, there you are Tony. I've just heard from the headmaster, and the caretaker. The school seems to be having some technical difficulties, so there'll be no more lessons today and everyone can go home early. Please sign out in the school office on your way out. I'm really sorry about this, children …'

Tony made his way home as fast as he could. This was not good. Not good at all.

7. MATHS, MYTHS AND MONSTERS

Back home, Tony headed straight for his kitchen. He needed to launch the *Invincible* as soon as possible, but when he got there he found the place in disarray. The washing machine was pulled out into the middle of the room and there were tools everywhere. Oily rags were draped over the cupboard where the button was hidden. Suddenly, Chris's head appeared from behind the washing machine.

He was lying down amongst the pipes with a spanner in his hand.

'Ahh, Tony. You're back early. Everything OK? I'm trying to fix the washing machine. It's the third time it's broken this week. I've just put the kettle on, would you like a hot chocolate?'

Tony looked around in panic whilst Chris walked over to the kettle and started fiddling with the switch.

'Um, yes, that would be lovely, Chris ...'

'Should have boiled by now ... what?! I don't believe it – now THIS has broken too, and I don't have my electrical tools here!'

Quickly, Tony said, 'Why don't you pop to your van, Chris. You might have some tools in there.

'Good idea Tony, Thanks. I can't stand things not working properly.'

As soon as he heard Chris walk down the hall, Tony ran back to the kitchen, moved the rags to one side, found the button and **CLICK** pressed it. There was no time to lose.

Back on board the *Invincible,* the Computer started up.

'Tony, good, you're back. Whilst you have been busy in school I have been doing some work of my own. Firstly, some calculations.'

'Some what? Quick, we haven't got long!'

'Sums, Tony. As Dot grows, its appetite is going to grow too, massively. He has already caused havoc with small powered items around your house and school, but if it multiplies and grows again, a big meal could mean diaster...'

+1x357+400x3456675/234455 = DISASTER!!

'Yeah, tell me about it!'

'**AND I have also found what could possibly be a reference to the alien life form you call "Dot".**'

'Wait, I thought you said there were no records of it in any of your data banks.'

'**Correct, Master Spears, but this isn't from the Encyclopaedia Galactica, it is from an ancient text from a long-extinct civilisation. It was carved into a lump of stone found floating in space many years ago—**'

'OK! What does it say?' cut in Tony.

'It describes many things, amongst them an unusual creature called the "Aankhen":

'IF THEY COME YOU MUST RUN. SMOOTH IS GOOD, BUT NOT SPIKEY. FEAR THE COLOUR BLUE, EVEN MORE THE COLOUR RED. DO NOT LET THEM GROW. IF THEY GROW THEY WILL EAT, AND EVERYTHING WILL END.

'And there are drawings, which I'm showing on my screen now.'

Tony looked at the images on the screen. He'd recognise those three eyes anywhere.

ΔΔΝΚΗΕΝ

'Computer, that bit about "everything will end"… out in space, Dot almost ate a star up completely. What would happen if Dot nibbled or ate our closest star, the sun?'

'Almost certainly, it would mean the end of all life on Earth …'

A serious look came over Tony's face.

'OK, computer. I have a plan.'

Behind him, he could feel the familiar tingling zinging sensation of Dot approaching.

'We launch immediately, for one last game of galaxy tag …'

8. ENDGAME

Within seconds Tony was at the helm of the *Invincible*, blasting into outer space.

And behind him, trailing in his jetstream, was Dot, no doubt looking forward to another game of tag.

'Computer, I need to have all your power at my disposal. When I say NOW I want you to set course for Earth, super-mega-duper speed. This time we need to return to Earth alone.

Now, Computer, NOW!'

the *Invincible's* engines roared. The speed was so great that Tony was flattened back into his seat.

'Uh-oh, Dot's following me, Computer.'

'Yes, Master Spears. I would imagine it thinks this is part of your game.'

'But, Computer, I don't want Dot to follow us. We need to outrun it. Initiate extreme evasive manoeuvres!'

Travelling at super-mega-duper speed, the ship began flipping and spinning, weaving this way and that. All the time followed by Dot.

'It's keeping up! Computer,
what should I do?'

'I don't think it will be easy to leave
Dot. You saved it, and have nurtured it,
and now it depends on you. As you said, you
think it likes you and sees you as its friend.
You have a responsibility to him, Tony.'

'But, Computer, he can't stay with me on
Earth. He could end everything!'

'That is true, Tony, but I do not think
this is the right way to solve this problem.'

And Tony began to relax his grip on the
throttle.

'You're right, Computer, he is my friend.

This is no way to finish this.' Tony sat there thinking while Dot bobbed and bounced outside the viewing port, tentacles jiggling.

'Computer, the ancient stone described the Aankhen as "THEY". That must mean there are more of them out there, mustn't it?'

'Correct, Master Spears.'

'So that's what I need to do – find his family. I never thought of it before, but he must have a family like me somewhere. They must be terribly worried about him.'

'It is possible, Master Spears.'

'Computer, sometimes things have to change, don't they?'

'It would appear so, Tony. Shall I set course for home?'

And so the *Invincible* zoomed its way back to earth with Dot following behind.

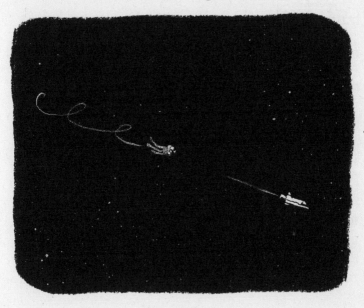

9. THE BLUES AND THE REDS

Over the next few weeks, life began to get busier and busier for Tony. As Dot grew, he needed more attention. He wanted to play more, he did more poos and, most troublesome of all, his appetite was increasing and he had started to snack on just about anything. The toaster, the washing machine, and all Tony's toys that had batteries in had been drained of power. Twice, the South East train network

went down, and Tony had his suspicions Dot
was responsible.

The only thing that Tony was sure about
was that he needed to find the rest of Dot's
family.

But he had spent hours scanning galaxy
after galaxy and he couldn't find them anywhere.

**'Wherever the Aankhen live, they do not
want to be found. There is a reason why
these creatures have never been discovered,'**
said the Computer. **'I have calculated the**

6+7

chances of us finding the alien's family to be 1 in 9 hundred and 99 billion zillion trillion ... At the rate we are going, it will take at least 99 squillion billion zillion trillion millennia to search the whole multiverse, and we do not have that long ...'

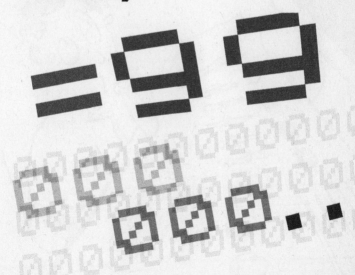

'OK, Computer, I get the picture. But we've got to do something! Dot can't stay with us on Earth. He must have a family somewhere. We just need to find them.'

Alongside this, Tony had also noticed another change in Dot. His colour had been getting gradually bluer and bluer, with occasional angry red spikes.

The computer had noticed this too.

'Tony, I think Dot is ill. I have been monitoring him closely but I do not understand what is ailing him. We have been

feeding him, and taking him to black holes
so he can emit waste, and you have been
playing with him, doing all the things that baby
infants require, but his colouring is wrong.'

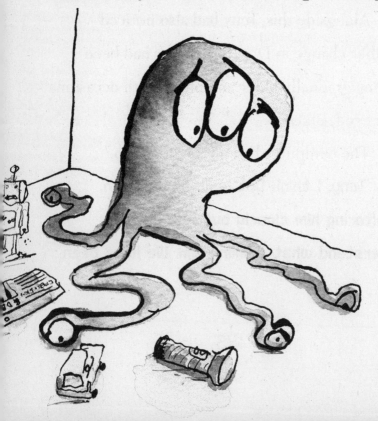

'I've been thinking about this too, Computer. There's one thing we haven't been able to give him.'

'What's that, Master Spears?'

'Love, Computer. I can give him friendship, but not love like a family, or a mum or a dad, or a brother or sister. I know somewhere out there Dot has a family, and he is missing them. Terribly. We just need to find them, that's all.'

And so the term progressed and all the time Dot got bigger …

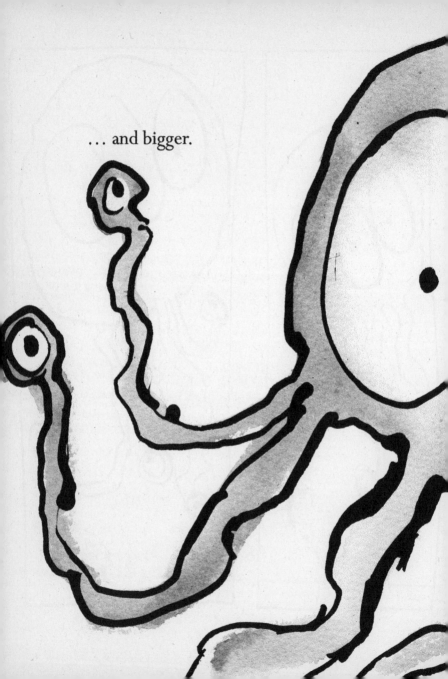

... and bigger.

There were many close calls where Dot would wake and turn red, so Tony would play an extra-long game with him to cheer him up.

Once, Dot nibbled a star in the constellation of Orion, causing Betelgeuse to prematurely supernova. Tony had been very cross with Dot about that. Thankfully nobody was hurt, but Tony knew he was running out of time. It was also hard work looking after big Dot, so by the time the term had come round to the project presentations, Tony hadn't had time to prepare anything at all.

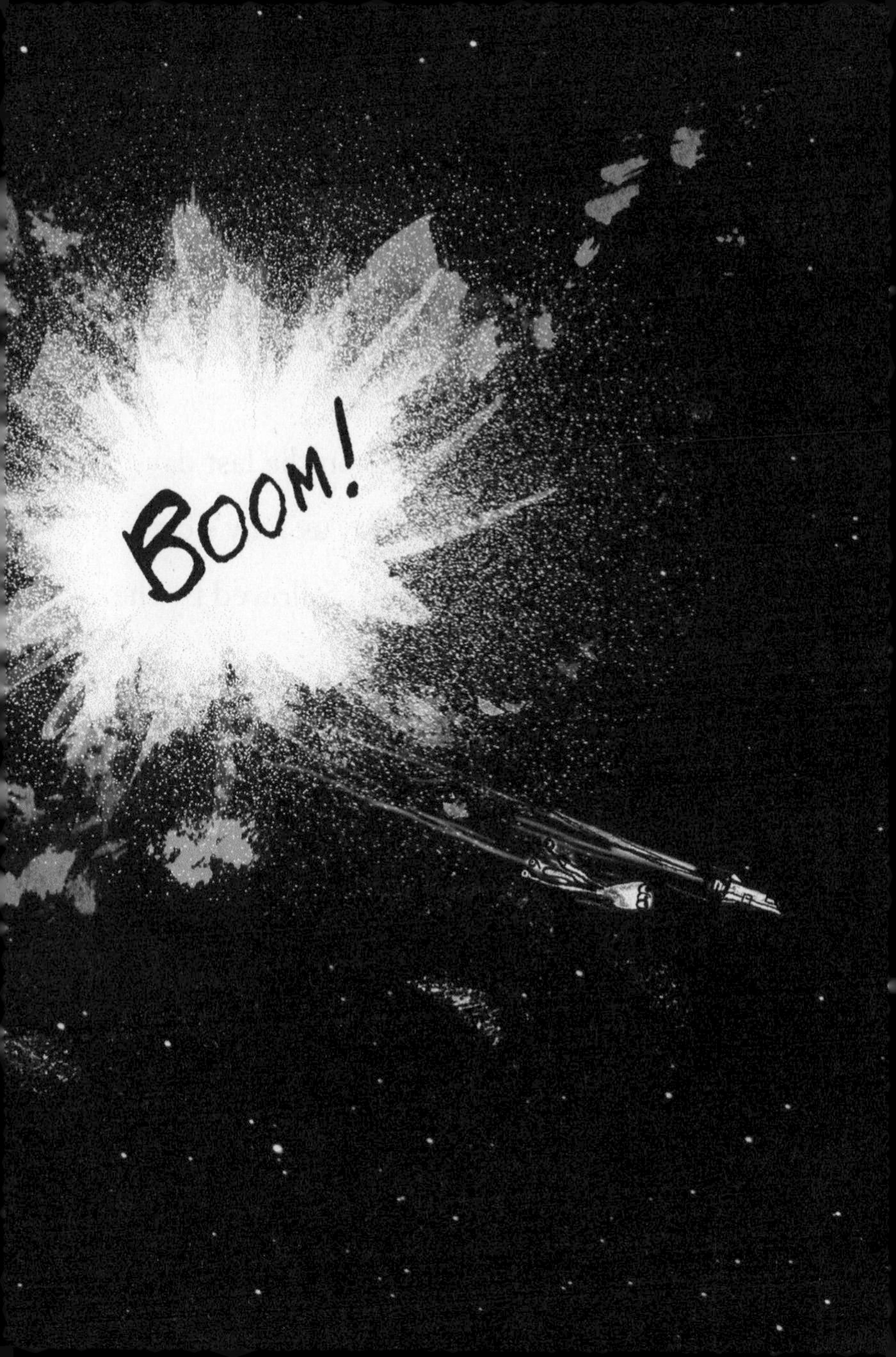
BOOM!

10. THE
PRESENTATION

There was always a big buzz on the last day
of school, even more so today as Tony's class
had their projects to present, followed by the
disco.

In his classroom, all the children made
their presentations. Brian had brought his
huge tank made out of shoe boxes and papier
maché. Inside it were sheets of paper with tank
facts written on them. Bertrand performed a

demonstration of a real flying rocket using soda
powder and elastic bands.

And then it was Tony and Chandra's turn to talk to the class. Except Chandra wasn't there …

'Right, Tony, if you'd like to start your presentation by yourself, I think Chandra will be here in a minute.'

'Um, OK,' said Tony.

'Our joint presentation is all about babies. And, erm…'

Tony held up some of the sheets of baby pictures they had made together.

'Every animal begins life as a baby — caterpillars, lion cubs, even humans like us. We all began life in the same way … small …'

Just then the door opened.

'Oh, fabulous, here she is now,' said Mr Simpson.

And the class spun round to see Chandra walk in, holding a little wriggling thing, followed by her mum.

'And here we have a real life human baby, my little brother, Ansu,' announced Chandra proudly.

The class got out their seats and crowded round. Tony had never looked at a baby before, not a real one, not properly. The first thing that

struck him was how small it was. Its face was

beaming, looking from one person to another.

Some of the girls went *ahh*. Some of the boys pretended they weren't interested, but everyone was fascinated. Chandra reached out her hand and Ansu's tiny one came to meet it, grasping her little finger.

This went on for some time until a strange look came over the baby, like a cloud casting a shadow across a sunny picnic, and then his mouth opened wide, his eyes closed, and the wailing started. Getting louder, and LOUDER and LOUDER !

Chandra's mum came back into the classroom. 'Oh, Ansu whatever is the matter? I could hear you down the corridor, come here.' And she picked him up and soothed him.

'WELL, THANK YOU VERY MUCH FOR BRINGING IN ANSU, CHANDRA,' shouted Mr Simpson above the wailing. 'What a lovely way to support the work you've been doing. Everyone say GOODBYE TO ANSU.'

As the wailing continued down the corridor, Chandra leaned across to Tony. 'No need to look so shocked, Tony, it's just what babies do! Little Ansu just wanted his mum. He couldn't see her, so he made a big noise so she'd come and find him. All animals do it. You'll get used to it.'

'Well, that just about draws the term to a close. Thank you for all your wonderful presentations. The disco will start in one hour so if you're going home to get changed, please do so now, or if you've brought your outfit with you, you can get changed here and go to the hall to help with the preparations.' Said Mr Simpson. 'I'll see you all in an hour for the disco!'

11. THE DISCO

As the class chattered their way to their school bags and outfits, Tony spoke to Chandra.

'Thanks, Chandra, that was brilliant, really brilliant. But listen, I've forgotten my outfit so I'll have to run home to get changed. I'll see you at the disco soon.'

Tony ran all the way home, puffing and panting his way straight up the stairs and into his bedroom. But as he darted into his room, he immediately slipped right over – SPLAT – into a huge pile of glittery sticky green goop. 'DOT!' exclaimed Tony.

His communicator buzzed.

'Ah, Tony, I'm glad you have come home, I've been trying to contact you. Dot has emitted a large quantity of waste that needs cleaning up before your mum comes home ... but I have also been tracking an extreme build-up of unusual energy within him. Something very big is about to happen, I estimate within the next 27 minutes.'

'Yes, don't worry,' replied Tony as he wiped the glittery-goop up. 'I've got it, I know what we need to do! Well, it was Chandra's idea really, although she didn't know it, but she gave me the idea ...'

'Tony, you are not making sense. Please speak slowly and logically ... we do not have much time. Dot will be waking soon and the energy build-up is becoming faster and faster. We don't know what this means. Remember what the ancient stone said: fear the red, it could mean the end of everything.'

'Yes, sorry. Right, we need to find Dot's family, don't we, in like … 27 minutes or less, or it could mean the end of everything …'

'That is correct, Master Spears. Actually, 25 minutes and 22 seconds …'

'Yes, yes, well, I know how we can do it!'

As Tony was talking, he could see the clock on his communicator steadily counting down, in minutes and seconds …

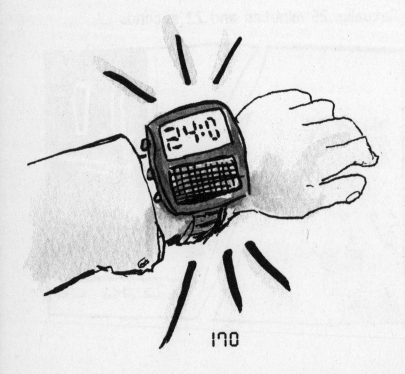

'Well, Dot needs to get back to his mum and dad, right?'

'That is correct, Master Spears. But as I have said, we will never be able to search the remainder of the multiverse in 24 minutes and 49 seconds ...'

'Yeah, but we're looking at it all wrong. I don't think we can ever find Dot's mum, but ... SHE can find US.'

'I don't understand, Master Spears.'

'What will the mother, or the family of any animal, always respond to? The cry of their young, of course, of their babies. It's what mothers and fathers do, whether they're sheep, dogs, birds, whatever. They always do the same thing, look after their young. And if their young cry, they go to them.

'Every time Dot cries, we've been feeding him, or playing with him, trying to keep him quiet so he doesn't cry.

'Perhaps we should let him cry, just for a little bit, let him cry for his mum. If she hears him she'll come to find her son, I know it! If Dot misses his mum, I know his mum will be missing Dot too!

'Listen, I've got to go back to the disco at school now. Let me know as soon as Dot wakes up. I'll run back home, by which time Dot will have done enough crying to alert his mum. Then I can keep him happy until his mum arrives and takes him home to wherever these "Aankhen" live.'

'I see the logic in this plan, Tony, but there are many uncertainties —'

'Look, we don't have a choice, do we? This is the best I can come up with right now … Remember, call me as soon as he wakes up and

I'll come straight back.'

'Affirmative. I will monitor Dot's status and keep you updated via your communicator. I estimate it will take you 5 minutes to walk back to the school disco, quicker if you run.'

Tony ran back to the disco.

With all the running, Tony was even more
out of breath when he arrived back at school.
Outside, he could hear music coming from
the hall. The curtains were drawn with flashes

of light peeping through the gaps. There were lots of children dressed up outside, and then suddenly Tony remembered he had forgotten to get changed into his outfit, or even get cleaned up after slipping in Dot's goop!

Suddenly the main doors opened and Chandra appeared.

'Hi, Tony, I saw you arrive. Wow, well done on your outfit.'

Confused, Tony looked down at his glittery-green-goop-spattered uniform.

'A super-green sparkly alien boy! It looks fantastic – I think you might win a prize with that. What on Earth did you make it from? I don't know how you can bear being THAT sticky, but it does look great!'

Inside the school hall it was a carnival

179

of colourful creatures. Giant beetles, bears, robots and more, some of them yelling across the across the room to congratulate him on his outfit. 'Hey, Tony, good effort mate!'

181

With the dance floor filled with such an outlandish cast, Tony began to feel less aware of being covered head to toe in Dot's goop.

Over to one side, Tony could see where the DJ had set up her turntables to play the tunes. She was wearing a bright pink clown wig with enormous sunglasses and looked suspiciously like one of the teachers, Miss Stephenson.

Tony kept glancing at his watch.

22 minutes.

21 minutes.

20 minutes.

Dot should be waking up soon, surely. This is the longest sleep he's had yet.

Then Chandra said, 'I love this song, do you want to dance, Tony?'

And before Tony had time to answer, she grabbed his hand and pulled him onto the dance floor.

They began bopping to the music.

'Thanks for bringing in Ansu for the project, Chandra. It was a brilliant idea. It's helped me a lot.'

'Don't mention it, Tony. I think you're doing really well. I was a bit worried before my little brother came along, but now it's fine.

Babies can be a lot of fun, you know. And when you've tired of them, you can always hand them back to their mum. That's what I do, anyway!'

'You're so right, Chandra.'

Suddenly Tony's watch buzzed.

He put it to his ear so he could hear above the sound of the disco.

'Computer, COMPUTER, are you there?'

'Tony – Tony – come in Tony – Dot has woken up but we have a BIG problem ... most unexpected ... Dot has multiplied ... HUGE size ... danger levels ... HIGH ...'

Suddenly the Computer's voice turned into crackle and then disappeared completely.

Then several things happened at the same time. Firstly, the lights and music cut out and for a fraction of a second there was complete silence before the whole room lit up with a light show of dancing colours; blues and indigos, accompanied by a low pulsing noise.

Tony stopped dancing whilst all around him the children started jumping in time to the beat.

'Wow, Crazy Em's discos are the best. I've never a seen light show like this.'

189

But Tony had moved away from Chandra and stopped dancing.

It must be Dot. These colours, they're the ones he makes when he's sad.

The pulsing beat became louder and the colours faster and faster, shifting downwards through the spectrum, becoming redder and redder.

Tony tried shouting into his communicator. But the screen was blank.

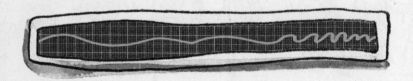

'Tony, this song is great! I wonder what Crazy Em is going to mix in now?' Meanwhile, Crazy Em and Mr Simpson were at the decks flicking switches, trying to work out what was going on.

And then it happened.

For an instant, everything in the room went red, as if lit from inside …

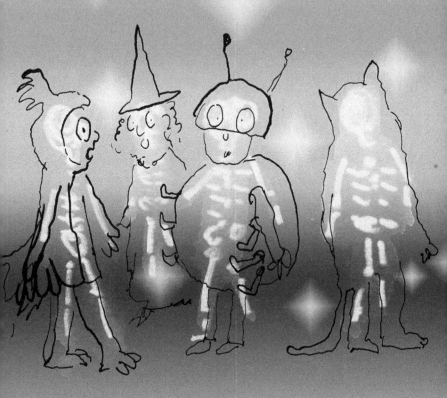

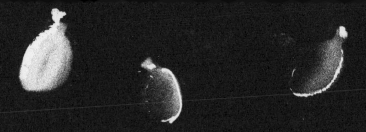

and then pitch blackness, as all the power in the

town went at once.

Balloons dropped from the ceiling, POP POP POP, as children stepped on them in the dark.

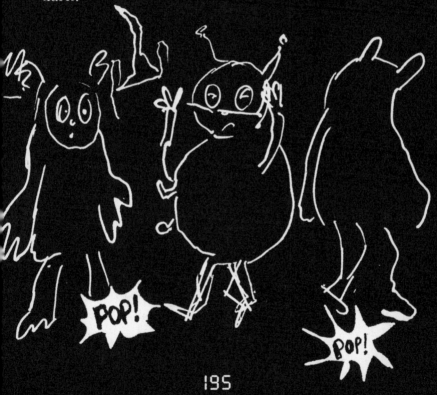

'Here, take this,' said Tony as he loosened
the strap on his communicator and handed
it to Chandra, pushing the LIGHT button,
and flicking it up to MAX setting as he did
so. Thankfully, it seemed to be working, as
immediately a globe of warm light surrounded
her.

'But, Tony, this is your *special* watch.'

'I know, but it's also a torch. Look, it's lit up almost the whole room, so you can see. Here take it. Find Mr Simpson and keep this button pushed to MAX setting. You and the rest of the children can stay here until the power comes back on, and I'm back.'

'Wait, where are you going?'

'I've got something I have to do. Remember the MAX setting. And try not to press anything else!'

197

12. THE SKY AT NIGHT

Outside, it was raining. Behind him, the warm glow from his communicator was lighting the school hall. Tony caught sight of a glowing red tentacle trailing along the ground, and spun round to see a now enormous Dot slumped across the school roof. Draping down from his body were hundreds and hundreds of tentacles, each one ending in an eyeball.

Tony found his way to the eyeball nearest him and cupped it in his hand, holding it close to his face.

'Dot, I'm so sorry, I didn't mean to upset you. I am your friend, I will always be your friend, but you need your family, your mum and dad, wherever they are.'

As he talked, more and more eyeballs tentacled their way towards Tony's face until he was faced with a sea of eyeballs, all staring at him.

Tony tried to put everything he could into his returning gaze. All the complicated feelings trapped inside him, he tried to pour them outwards through his eyes. He could feel Dot's look boring deep inside him, but this time, because he was not faced with three eyes, but hundreds of eyeballs, it seemed to have even more power. Gradually he could feel Dot's mood change, and slowly his red and blue colours were replaced by the more familiar orange and golden yellows.

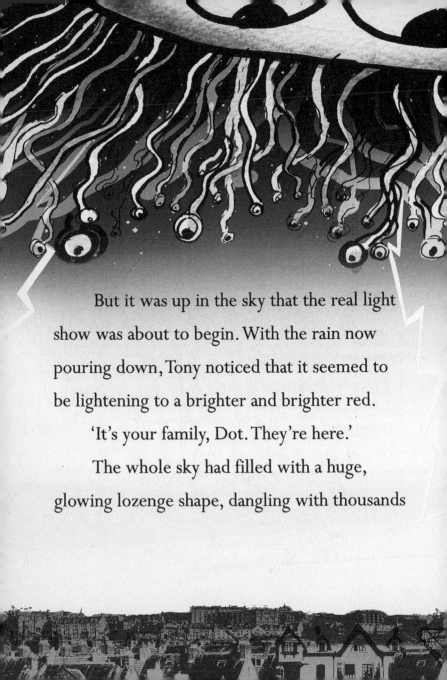

But it was up in the sky that the real light
show was about to begin. With the rain now
pouring down, Tony noticed that it seemed to
be lightening to a brighter and brighter red.

'It's your family, Dot. They're here.'

The whole sky had filled with a huge,
glowing lozenge shape, dangling with thousands

of tentacles like Dot's. In the centre of the
lozenge were three eyes, each, larger than the
moon, all three fixed on Tony.

And then across the whole sky came a
series of flicking pinpricks like embers from
a fire. Loud cracks of pink lightning started
shooting down in angry flashes.

The three giant eyes continued looking at Tony, and then across the rest of the town. The lightning cracks turned a deeper and deeper red. And Tony remembered the ancient writing the computer had found.

FEAR THE COLOUR BLUE, EVEN MORE THE COLOUR RED.

Tony didn't notice that his clothes were soaked through.

'Dot, you have to let your mum know that we are friends …

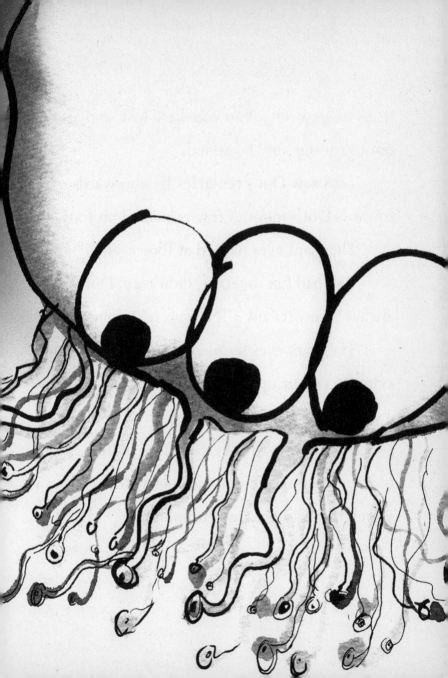

that I helped you when you were lost, and also not to eat our sun' he added.

Tony saw Dot's tentacles flow upwards towards Dot's mum. A few remained on Tony.

The giant eyes flashed at Tony again.

'We had fun together, didn't we, Dot? You'll always be my friend. I'll always remember you.'

The giant eyes seemed to be softening, the crimson colour up above seemed to be lessening, and then, with one huge unexpected bounce, Dot flew up into the sky, tentacles trailing, blurring into the enormous pulsing form above which then disappeared completely.

209

13. THE STORM

Back at the school, some of the parents had arrived on foot with flashlights. More lightning bolts zigzagged down from the black skies overhead. The storm seemed to be worsening.

Suddenly a familiar face appeared out of the watery gloom.

'Tony, TONY?! Is that you? Thank goodness I've found you. Quick, we need to get home, it's your mum, the baby is coming.'

Chris grabbed Tony's hand and together

they ran through the streets which flowed
like rivers from the rain. Apart from the noise
of the storm, it was eerily quiet. No traffic.
Eventually they got to Tony's flat, and a figure
with another flashlight greeted them in the hall.

'Oh, well done, Chris, you found him.
This way … my name's Lou by the way, I'm one
of the midwives. She's OK, Chris. Don't worry.
Everyone is OK.'

Tony and Chris slowed as they reached his
mum's bedroom. The door was half ajar and a
warm candlelit glow crept around it. Outside,

they could hear the rain hammering against the window. Very gently, Tony pushed the door open and entered, followed by Chris with his hand on Tony's shoulder.

Tony's mum was lying down in bed.

When she saw him enter, she looked up. 'Tony, I heard about everything you did at school today. I'm so proud of you. We've been busy at home too. Tony, meet your sister.'

Tony looked closely and there, cuddled into his mum, was a little screwed-up face with tiny hands and bunched fists.

Gently, his mum lifted the tiny lifeform towards Tony, and as his hands went out to carefully cradle her head, she moved her gaze towards him, and Tony looked into her big glassy eyes.

'Ahh, Tony, you're a natural with her. I knew you would be. Tony, meet Tara.'

And, suddenly, throughout the room there came a warm orange glow — and Tony felt the familiar tingling-zinging sensation of Dot, like

Dot was congratulating him.

And something more.

He suddenly felt like he'd done something good.

He had saved a life, a life that would otherwise have been lost, and he had reunited a family.

Then, as quickly as it came, the glow was gone. Suddenly the lights began to flicker and come back on.

Chris jumped up from where he had been kneeling by the bed and said, 'Hey, my phone's working again. Great — at last I can take a

family picture!'

217

14. EPILOGUE

The next morning, Tony woke up early.

Somehow in the night everything had started working again — all Tony's toys, the toaster, the washing machine, everything.

He tiptoed past his mum's bedroom and peeped in. She was fast asleep in bed, cradling Tara.

Outside, the sun was shining, drying up the water from the night before. Tony couldn't put his finger on it, but somehow the world looked different. He had saved the world, but more important than that he was a big brother.

Aankhen – *a species of energetic lifeforms discovered by Tony Spears in AD 2018.*

'Computer, do you think I will ever see Dot again?'

'I can't say, Master Spears, but there was a bond formed between you that I cannot explain. I would call it friendship, and according to my understanding of such things, once formed, it is very difficult to break.'

'Yeah, thanks Computer.'

Tony's thoughts were broken by a strange sound. A sound he had never heard before in his house, the sound of a tiny baby crying.

'I think my baby sister has woken up, I'd better go. She might need me. See you soon, Computer.'

'Affirmative, Master Spears.'